Guitar

Shop

Told By

LaVeL Regine

CScottGroupInc.

2020

This Page Left Blank Intentionally

Scott Publishing House

A subsidiary of CScottGroupInc.

Copyright © 2020 LaVeL Regine

See more from author at:

www.lavel.uk

ISBN-13: 97809854322-3-2

Contents

Chapter 1

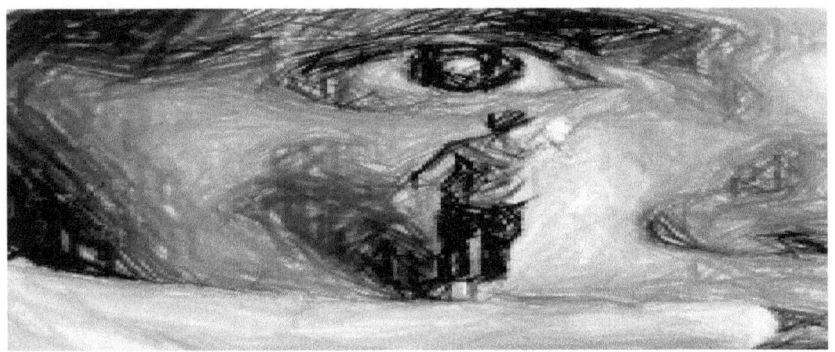

Consultation

To be honest, I did not know what to expect. In fact, I was turned off by the whole idea. The only reason I went was because it was a condition of my release. I had to maintain on going care with a professional. To make matters worse, I did not even get to choose that professional. Instead, I was issued one. As if these types of professionals should or even could be selected in that fashion.

Her name was Dr. Vivian Ochoa. I obsessively thought to myself for days prior to our first session about the uniqueness of her name. I found it to be just as unique as the situation I had found myself in. I believe it added to the anxiety I had about going in the first place. I was not sure what to expect.

I assumed she was Hispanic given her last name. However, her Americanized first name contradicted that idealism. Then I thought that perhaps she had married a Hispanic man and that is how she acquired her last name. I am not prejudice of Hispanic men but for some reason a part of me did not want her to be married to one.

Honestly, I do not know why I felt that way. Perhaps it was her first name, Vivian. Which at first glance gave me the impression that she may have been of ethnic origins. Maybe even African American or a combination of. Though predominantly, African American in my mind.

The truth is it really should not have mattered. What difference should have it made to me? I did not even know her so why did I even care? It was these notions that led me to follow through with the appointment. On one hand, I wanted to know the mystery behind her name. Then on the other, the fact that I was obsessing over something that should not have concerned me made me realize that something was not right.

I arrived at the appointment twenty-five minutes early. What a mistake that was because for the entire twenty - five minutes the ongoing commentary in my head was trying to convince me to leave. It was that commentary that ultimately made me stay. Then it was interrupted by a soft subtle voice.

"Mr. Kingston," the voice called out. "Michael Kingston," it called out again after no response answered the first call.

I was hesitant to respond. I believe this was the case because I was trying to feel out who she was. As she stood there in the door defying all my preconceived assumption, I admired her. She was not of ethnic background. She was not African American nor

Hispanic. She was not even of European decent. Instead, she appeared to be Native American.

She was tall and slender. Her skin was fair but still pigmented. In fact, it was not too much lighter than my own. Her hair was long, straight, and even blacker than mine. Her eyes were golden and had an orangish tint to them as they peered out into the lobby.

"Mr. Michael Kingston," She called out once more seeming as if she was losing patience.

Just as she turned to exit the lobby something took over me and words fell from my mouth.

"Michael Kingston.... yes, I am here," I called out grabbing her attention.

"Well... Mr. Kingston, I almost gave up on you," She replied as I stood to my feet and made my way to her.

Upon my arrival she extended her hand and greeted me.

"Mr. Kingston my name is Dr. Ochoa, but you can call me Vivian," She said as our hands made contact.

"It is a pleasure to meet you Vivian and please... just Michael is fine," I replied.

"Very well then... Michael it is," Vivian agreed. "Right this way Michael," she went on as she led the way down the hallway to her office.

Upon entering her office, I got a glimpse into who she really was. The office was very small and modest. It was no more than one hundred fifty square feet. Within it there were only a few things. There were two chairs. One in which was behind a desk with a computer on top of it and the other positioned directly across from it.

In the right corner behind the desk there was a small bookcase which stored several psychology books, a few files, and a printer. That was the sum of the collective in her office. Not much to go on as far as formulating a generalization of her character. I guess I had my work set out for me as I would have to go about it the good old fashion way, conversation.

Vivian wasted no time she just seemed to dive right into things.

"Okay Michael, with all my new patients I like to start off with an assessment to see if in fact we are a good fit for one another," Vivian explained as she proceeded to place a voice recorder on top of her desk between the two of us. "I am going to record this intake as a reference that we may elect to utilize in the future given we establish we are a good fit," She went on in a professional manner. "Is that alright with you Michael," She asked before starting the recorder?

"Sure, I am okay with that," I replied.

Vivian then proceeded to press record and the session had officially started.

"So, Michael if you would state your full name for the record," Vivian insisted.

"My name is Michael Jamerson Kingston," I stated for the record.

"Now if you would Michael tell me what brings you in to see someone like me," Vivian inquired.

"Well... to be honest it was ordered per the terms of my release from the Memorial Medical Behavioral Health facility. I was picked up and placed there against my will," I explained.

"Against your will... if you would Michael elaborate on that," Vivian suggested.

"What do you mean elaborate," I asked in a confused tone?

"Well, tell me the circumstance that led up to you being apprehended against your will if you would please," Vivian explained.

"Oh, okay... it's a funny story actually I was in my home minding my own business when I heard a knock at the door. When I answered the door there were cops and paramedics standing on my front porch requesting to enter my home. They said they received an anonymous call where the implication of my mental health was of concern," I eagerly ranted on.

'Okay, so someone was concerned about your mental health... any idea why that may have been the case Michael," Vivian asked?

"I am sure it was that nosey Mrs. Jenkins... Ever since her husband died last fall, she has been all in my personal space," I explained. She really started prying when Jill and the kids left... asking all type of question and what not," I went on. I guess the fact that I started seeing and talking to people that weren't actually there didn't help... or at least her husband Phil," I said then paused briefly to recollect on the transpiring of the events I had just explained.

The room momentarily filled with silence. I found myself slipping to the mental space that I had come to call Astro World. I was a bit taken by the fact that Vivian did not intervene. Instead, she just sat there and watch my every move. Luckily, I caught and gathered myself before I slipped to deep into Astro World. I quickly regained my composure and continued where I left off.

"You see, I am not really sure why Phil came to me... But he did," I explained. "In fact, Phil came to me almost every day... It was almost as if he had never left," I went on. "I guess occasionally Mrs. Jenkins would overhear me and Phil conversing and caring on... I assume she was jealous," I suggested. "Then again, as the psychiatrist at Memorial Behavioral put it... I was talking to her dead husband," I got out before Vivian abruptly interjected.

"So, you believe that Mrs. Jenkins anonymously called the authorities and reported your talking to her deceased husband is that correct," Vivian asked?

"Well, that's my best guess anyways... I can't seem to come up with anything else," I replied.

"With that in mind Michael do you believe that if Mrs. Jenkins did in fact call the authorities that actions were valid given the circumstances," Vivian asked?

"Honestly, Vivian, I think Mrs. Jenkins should mind her own business... and you know what, Phil agrees," I replied.

"I see... Michael, is Phil here with us now," Vivian asked?

"No, I imagine he is home annoyed by his hag of a wife... He says he is working off old karma and that is why he is stuck there with her even after his death," I explained. I say he must have done something really horrible to accumulate karma that requires that sort of repayment," I continued as I left off an instinctual chuckle.

Vivian did not share my humor. Instead she asked in a stern tone, "Michael is Phil the only person you see in this context?"

In the back of my mind I knew at this point she was trying to shrink-wrap me. It did not bother me in the least bit. In fact, I found it to be very humorous. Considering the Psych at Memorial Behavioral had just recently diagnosed me as Schizophrenic. I did not see things getting any worse than that. Plus, I had already figured out the parameters that could land me back at Memorial Behavioral. If I were not feeling like hurting myself or anyone else, I could say just about anything and be okay. So, I told the truth.

"Yes, quite often actually," I boldly confessed.

"Michael do you recall the first encounter with someone in this context," Vivian asked?

"How could I forget the Guitar Man... I believe I first saw him when I was round seven years old," I explained. "Then I didn't know it but later I learned that the Guitar Man was in fact Apollo... the God of music," I continued. "He had a way of showing up at just the right time... you know, when things got tough," I went on. "He would come, and he would have a beautiful guitar with him that he would play for me," I said now wearing a warm smile upon my face.

Telling Vivian about Apollo brought back memories of the good times we had over the years. Apollo was one of my best friends. He was one of those friends you could always count on to lift you up even in your darkest hour. The room had filled with silence once more as I reminisced amongst myself. Again, my brief detour from the conversation did not seemed to bother Vivian at all. In fact, it was me who eventually broke the silence.

"You know, I haven't talked to Apollo in a while come to think of it... I guess He's been busy doing you know, Godly things," I said now waiting on a response from Vivian.

"Michael did Apollo ever tell you why he was visiting you," Vivian asked in a curious tone?

"Not that I recall... why do you ask," I investigated?

"Well, it just seems peculiar that the Greek God of Music choose to visit and befriend you... Perhaps he saw something special in you," Vivian suggested.

Her suggestion made me ponder. Perhaps Apollo did see something special in me that even I may have overlooked all these years. The wheels began to chirm in my mind. Before I could slip into another deep thought and the commentary in my mind, Vivian voice filled the silence in the room.

"Do you or have you ever considered playing the Guitar Michael," Vivian asked?

"I can't say that I have ever given it any real consideration... I mean, I have always been busy with life you know," I explained. "You know the bizarre thing about it is for a while I actually had a guitar," I went on.

"Really, so you had interest in the guitar and went out and bought one then could never find time to play it," Vivian asked in a curious tone?

"Not exactly, I didn't go out and buy the guitar.... I woke up one morning and it was there," I explained. "It was Apollo's Guitar... "There was a card left in the strings that read, use it wisely – Apollo," I continued. "I guess to me the idea of Apollo leaving his guitar behind suggested that he would not be coming around for a while... Perhaps that is why I never played it," I went on.

Silence once more briefly filled the room. This time it was Vivian that broke the silence.

"So, whatever became of this guitar Apollo gifted you," Vivian asked?

"Well, to be honest it is quite unfortunate... Jill and I came upon some hard times after we had Rachel, so I ended up hawking it for cash to get by," I explained in a regretful tone. "That was the last time I saw it... Perhaps, if I had it now, I would play it," I continued. "Given I have all this free time currently have on my hands... with the divorce and now being on leave from work," I went on.

"That is very unfortunate about Apollo's guitar Michael but maybe you could get a new guitar and play it,"

Vivian suggested. "Perhaps playing the guitar may bring you peace in your time of trial," She went on.

"Peace... In my time of trial," I replied in a sarcastic tone.

"Yes, peace in your time of trial," Vivian insisted. "It would take your mind off your divorce and your job for the time being... Perhaps it is exactly what you need right now," Vivian reiterated.

"Yeah you know you may be right... Maybe I will poke around a few Guitar Shops and see if I could find me a new guitar," I assured. "Maybe I will even get lucky and find Apollo's guitar and finally be reunited," I continued.

Though the idea of finding Apollo's guitar sounded good I knew there was a slim chance in doing so. However, thinking about it made me realize what a big mistake I made letting it go in the first place. I am now certain it is probably why I have not seen Apollo in so long. I am sure I must have offended him by pawning his guitar.

I knew what had to be done. Somehow, I had to find Apollo's guitar. However, I did not have the slightest idea on how to do that. Despite that, I was going to try.

"Well Michael we have reached our time for today," Vivian voice captured my attention before I slipped to far into thought. "The good news however is that I feel like we are a good fit and I would like to continue working with you if that is alright with you," She continued then waited on my response.

I was hesitant to respond because honestly, I was hoping she would say she did not think I needed any further care. Who was I kidding though? I had just told her I was friends with Apollo the Greek God of music. She must have thought I was completely out of my mind. Or at the least agreed with my current Schizophrenia diagnosis.

Despite all that, the reality was I was friends with Apollo. I am not sure how that was possible but for me somehow it was. Did that make me schizophrenic however, I guess that was up to the professionals. So, with that in mind I considered taking Vivian up on her offer.

"Vivian, I think it would be great for us to work together," I said in an optimistic tone.

"Fantastic Michael, I believe you will find that therapy can be a great resource in your life," Vivian assured. "We can start meeting every Tuesday at 1:00 P.M.," She continued.

"Okay, Tuesdays at 1:00 P.M. works for me," I confirmed.

"Great, then it is set... Tuesdays at 1:00 P.M.," Vivian re-confirmed. "So, I like to leave each session with something to build on for our next session which in this particular case I believe you going out and looking into getting a new guitar would be a great Idea... How do you feel about that Michael," Vivian suggested?

"I think that would be doable," I concurred.

"Well Michael it has been nice speaking with you... do take care and I will see you next Tuesday at 1:00 P.M.," Vivian said as her final farewell.

"Okay Vivian, thank you so much... and I will see you then," I replied as I exited her office.

As I made my way to my car, I noticed that I felt better after talking with Vivian. I began to reflect in my mind to pinpoint how it was possible. I pondered if it was something I had said or Vivian that stimulated the relief I was experiencing. Either way one thing was noted the relief felt good. I honestly felt, optimistic.

Chapter 2

Optimistic

The next morning, I felt as if I had a sense of renewed purpose. My first instinct was to contribute it to the great night of sleep I had. However, after further consideration I realized that I owed that great night of sleep to the session I had with Vivian. I mean, what a relief it turned out to be.

With that in mind, I figured at the least I owed it to her and myself to follow through on the little assignment she suggested. Honestly, I was eager to go shopping for guitars. I was even somewhat optimistic about finding Apollo's guitar. Though I knew it would not be an easy task, I knew it was possible. As is anything for that matter.

In good spirits, I breezed right through my morning routine. That which had prior been a drag. I even made breakfast and took the time to have it at the kitchen table. Something I had not done since Jill and the kids had moved out. I was very impressed with myself.

After breakfast I did not waste any time. I headed right out. There was a guitar shop less than a mile away from the house. It was called, Guitar Shop. It was the shop where I sold Apollo's guitar. I figured it to be the perfect place to start my search. Perhaps I would get lucky.

When I got to the Guitar shop upon entry, I was approached by one of the employees. He was tall and slim. He had a head full of dread locks and looked that of a stoner. Though when he spoke, he defied all the preconceived notions I had mentally made of him. His voice and his mannerism were very articulate. Perhaps even that of an intellectual.

"Welcome to the Guitar Shop sir my name is Max, and I will be you concierge," He proclaimed as he extended his hand out to greet me.

My hand met with his without thought. There was no denying that I was very excited to be there. It was evident in my optimistic tone.

"Well thank you so much Max the pleasure is all mine," I said as I took his hand into mine and gave it a firm shake.

Wearing a big smile that seemed to radiate through my eyes I went on,

"Max, my name is Michael, and I am in search of a guitar."

"Well, Michael you have definitely come to the right place if it is a guitar you are searching for," Max assured wearing a smile just as radiant as mine. "We have over six hundred guitars here in stock and we can get just about anything your heart desires if you don't find something to your liking in our current stock," Max went on.

"Actually Max, now that you mentioned it, I do have my heart set on a particular guitar," I replied. "You see a few years back I came in and I sold a guitar to you guys... is there any way to check and see if that guitar is available," I asked?

"Of course, let's take a walk over here to the computer and see what we can find," Max said as he proceeded to lead the way.

My level of optimism shot through the roof. There may have been hope still yet. Coupled with my optimism was a sense of excitement. There was something very nostalgic about being in the presence of all those guitars. I felt as if I was finally in pursuit of my true path in life.

Upon arrival to the computer Max wasted no time. He dove right into the search.

"Okay Michael, may I please have your last name so I can retrieve your customer profile," Max asked politely? "Your profile should have your complete history of transactions with us and we can hopefully find that guitar," He went on.

"Perfect, my last name is Kingston," I replied now eagerly anticipating the verdict.

Within a few strokes over the keyboard Max had results.

"Okay, I see here the transaction back on March 20, 2015 at 4:45 P.M. you came in and sold a Gibson L-1 Flat Top.... Mahogany Hollow body with a Mahogany neck and traditional rectangle bridge with a bone saddle," Max explained. "That's a pretty impressive guitar Michael," He went on. "Well, it looks like your guitar was so impressive that ten minutes after you sold it someone came in and bought it," Max continued.

As those last words fell from Max mouth my optimism was shattered. I felt as if I may have gotten my hope up prematurely. I guess Max saw the hope I had dissipate right before his eyes. It caused him to immediately try to cheer me up.

"'I'm' truly sorry Michael," Max sympathized. "Perhaps we have something similar to that here in stock that you will fall in love with," He went on optimistically.

I forced myself to stay positive. I gave a forced smile and promptly agreed.

"Yeah... you're right Max, perhaps you have something here I will fall in love with," I agreed. If you do not mind, I am just going to have a look around and if I see something that jumps out at me, I will come and grab you," I went on.

"Okay, and again sorry about the guitar Michael... If it every comes back through here you will be the first person I call," Max assured.

"Great, thank you so much.... I really would appreciate that," I said as I turned away to start my search.

"I'll be right over here if you need me," Max called out as I walked off.

As I made my way across the massive showroom, I was overwhelmed with guitar options. I mean guitars were everywhere. They covered every square inch of the walls.

Some were displayed across the floors. Some were even in boxes stacked up. There were too many options to choose from. However, I did not let that discourage me. I was determined.

Most of the ones on the walls were electric. Though they were all beautiful, I easily passed on them. I was not looking for an electric guitar. I figured if I could not have Apollo's guitar, I at least wanted one in its same caliber. An acoustic with maybe an electric pickup.

Then out of the corner of my eye I spotted in the far corner of the showroom a glass incased room that was filled with acoustic guitars. I eagerly made my way to it. When I opened the door to enter, the first thing I noticed was the smell. It was a mixture of fine fresh woods. An assortment ranging from fresh oaks to mahogany. If I had to guess what heaven smelled like, I would guess that smell was it.

Even in this room that was maybe a third of the showroom size did not fall short when it came to options. There must have been over two hundred guitars available to choose from. Again, I found myself overwhelmed as I still was not quite sure what I was looking for in a guitar. I mean I had only ever had one guitar in my entire life and did not know much about it. Hell, if I had I probably would not have sold it in the first place.

I figured the best thing I could do was pick a few up and see how they felt. Perhaps in doing so I would formulate some likes and dislikes and at least have something to go on. So, without bias I just picked up the nearest one to me and decided to give it a try. It was a Jett Black Martian OMC-X1E. I did not know much about it other than the name but figured it must be a decent guitar given its hefty price tag.

Holding it in my hand felt good. In that moment, I felt as if I was supposed to have a guitar in my hands. Perhaps not that particular guitar, but a guitar. I guess people call that an epiphany or something along those lines. Either way, it put a smile on my face.

I took a seat in a nearby stool and gave it a strum. I could feel the vibration the strings made radiating through my entire body. It felt good you know. Kind of tickled. So,

I gave it a few more strums. Before I knew it, I could not quit strumming it.

It was not until some young man entered the room before I stopped. He was a tall skinny fellow with peering eyes that sat behind round tea shade frames. From his attire I imaged that he must have been British. That was confirmed when he spoke. In a soothing monotone voice, he said,

"Well... sounds good old timer."

At first, I sat and admired him in silence. There was something very familiar about the young man, but I just could not place it. I guess my delayed response was not kosher. In lieu of it the young man quickly fired another remark in effort to stimulate a response.

"What's the matter ae... cat got your tongue," He went on in a sarcastic tone. "In all good manner when someone speaks to you the polite thing to do is say something back you know," He went on as he grabbed a guitar from the wall.

"Oh wow... my apologies you caught me lingering in a thought," I answered.

"No worries fellow, my name is John, and you are," He asked as he pulled up a stool next to me and took a seat.

'I'm Michael... Michael Kingston," I quickly replied as I extended my hand out to greet him.

"Oh now, you don't have to go and get all formal on me now Michael," John said. "Though I assure you it is a pleasure to make you acquaintance," He went on as he reached his hand out to mine and gave it a firm shake. "So, how long have you been playing that their guitar Michael," John asked?

"Well... this particular guitar only for a few minutes," I replied.

"Well now, you're a bit of a wise guy are you Michael," John asked.

"Not exactly, it just.... Do I know you I mean something about you seems very familiar," I replied?

"Yeah well you know I get that a lot Michael... Perhaps you knew me in a past life or something like that," John said. "Anyway, enough of the small talk let me see what you can do on that thing," He went on.

"Honestly, John, I don't know much I was just strumming around to get a feel for it before you came in," I explained. My therapist thought it might be a good idea to give it a try," I went on. "you know, to keep busy," I continued.

"Oh, I see... you're one of those screwy kinds of fellow ae," John said sarcastically and gave off a chuckle.

I could not help but laugh as well. I mean in a way he had made a point.

"Well, I wouldn't say that exactly... I mean not screwy but definitely disturbed at times," I explained.

"Oh, I got you, disturbed isn't all that bad," John said. "I've been disturbed a bit here and there I guess," He went on. Well any way how about you see if you can mimic what I do here... I'll try to show you something that will send you on your way to playing that there guitar," John explained. "I'm going to be playing two simple chords here Am and G," He went on as he began to strum the chords to "Working Class Hero".

It was then when I realized who he was. Then when he began to sing the lyrics to the chords it was confirmed. I was in the presence of greatness. Sir John Lennon was teaching me to play "Working Class Hero".

My first instinct was jump for joy and ask for an autograph. However, I held my composure because I did not want to interrupt his song. It sounded so beautiful. Then there was the fact that I did not want to address the elephant in the room. You know the fact that Sir John Lennon had been deceased for well over thirty plus years.

So instead, I just watched in marvel. For the entire four minutes John played and sang he had my undivided attention. Then when the song came to an end, I thirsted for more. I was captured in a glaring daze. Hypnotized by the surrealism of the occurrence. It was John's voice that pulled me from the subline.

"Okay then, let's see you give that a try now ae," John insisted.

My first thought was to refuse. I mean I had only watched him play the song once. Then most of that time I was captivated listening to the song. I was not really paying attention to how to play the song,

Despite that, something came over me. A dormant sense of confidence. So rather than cower from the request, I boldly stepped into myself and began to play. The chords sounded just as crisp as when John played them. This boosted my confidence and a sense of stillness bestowed me. So, I started to sing the lyrics to "Working Class Hero".

John smiled proudly as I played. I could see it in his demeanor that he was impressed by my playing. For the entire four minutes of that song I had John's undivided attention. It was then I realized, I did have something special. Perhaps it had been there all along. I just failed to own it.

At the end of the song John gave an applaud.

"Well then old timer I guess you can play that their guitar after all ae," John suggested.

"Yeah, I guess you are right," I concurred.

"Well, I think I have another in me," John said then proceeded to play "Real Love".

As he strummed his guitar and sang, I found myself in complete awe. It truly was an amazing thing to experience. Of course, I had my doubts that my theory was all in my imagination. Perhaps all this was just a very rare coincidence, or not. Either way, I was blown away.

At the end of the song John stood to his feet and rehung his guitar.

"I think I will have a cigarette now," John said as he made his way to the door.

Momentarily, I was in a state of shock. I did not want whatever was occurring to end just yet. Though, I could not move nor speak. I guess that is where the concept left speechless derived from. As John walked out the door, I forced myself to pull it together. I jumped to my feet rehung my guitar and proceeded to follow him.

"Hey John, wait up man," I called out hoping to capture Johns attention.

When John turned to me, he had a cigarette hanging from his lips. It was then I knew for sure that he was the real Sir John Lennon. There was no doubt in my mind.

"Yeah," He called out.

"I think I will join you... if you don't mind," I said.

"Sure, old timer," John replied then turned and lead the way out of the Guitar Shop.

When we made it to the parking lot John lit the cigarette that was in his lip as we approached a distinctive 1964 Rolls-Royce Phantom V. He reached into the back seat and pulled out a guitar. It was a Gibson L-1 Flat Top Mahogany Hollow body with a Mahogany neck and traditional rectangle bridge with bone saddle. It looked exactly like Apollo's guitar.

"Hey that's a nice guitar," I said fighting the urge to mention Apollo's guitar.

"Yeah, it plays well," John replied modestly. "It was a gift from a dear friend you know," He went on as he took the cigarette from his lips and stuck it between the string of the guitar at the top of the fret board.

He then proceeded to strum the chords to "No Body Loves You When Your Down and Out". Shortly after, He began to sing the lyrics. It truly was a majestic sight. The lyrics to that song really touched me. It made me think of Jill and the kids.

By the end of that song, I was John's biggest fan. I decided not to mention the fact that I knew who he was. I figured the mystery of it all made it that much more significant. It was as if, I got to visit with an angel.

We said our goodbyes and went our separate ways. Though on the short ride home, John lingered in my mind. I wanted to deny it happening. I could have very easily accounted the experience to my recent diagnosis. Though, something would not allow it. That something was John.

Every time I tried to convince myself it was a hallucination; I could hear his voice serenading me. Those soft simple chords strumming beneath his soul bridging lyrics. His remarkable fully developed personality being influenced by his purified integrated soul. A true artist. That night as I laid in bed, it was that voice that put me to sleep.

Chapter 3

Validation

Though I slept well, I anticipated getting back to the Guitar shop. I guess despite my better judgment and intuition, I was still harboring a bit of doubt about meeting Sir John. I figured one way to eradicate that doubt was to go back to the Guitar shop. If John came a second time, then there was no denying it. I was so eager to prove myself right or wrong, I skipped my morning routine and headed straight out.

When I arrived at the Guitar Shop, they were just opening. I figured I would wait in the car a few minutes to give them time to open properly. While waiting in the car a part of me was hoping I would see John pull up in his psychedelic Rolls-Royce. Unfortunately, that did not happen. Fifteen minutes had gone by and I was still the only car in the lot.

Though John did not pull up while I was waiting, I was still quite optimistic that he would show up eventually. So, I went inside. I figured I still needed a guitar anyway so since I was at the guitar shop might as well try and find one. Upon entry I was once again greeted by Max.

"Welcome back my friend," Max said invitingly displaying a warm smile. "Finding the right guitar takes time Michael so don't feel rushed or pressured," He went on. "Once you pick it up it will speak to you... so pick as many up as you need to," he continued.

I was impressed that he remembered my name. I mean he must see hundreds of people a day in his line of work. The fact that he did remember my name made me feel welcomed and comfortable doing just as he suggested. It even made me momentarily forget I was there to validate jamming out with Sir John.

"Well thanks Max... you sure do know how to make someone feel welcomed," I replied.

"Sure thing, Michael," Max said now blushing. "Well, you know your way around and keep in mind if you need me, I am always eager to help," He went on.

"Perfect, I think I am going to start off in the acoustic room... I will come and grab you if I need you," I assured Max as we parted ways.

When I made it to the acoustic room I was once more greeted by that beautiful smell as I entered. It warmed my heart and soul. That smell paired with the sight of all those beautiful guitars was enough to make anyone want to play in my opinion. The first one that caught my eyes was the one John had played yesterday.

It was a Gibson J-160E. Though primarily it was an acoustic guitar it did have electric pick up. I took the guitar from the wall took a seat in a nearby stool and proceeded to strum. My first thought was that once I began to play perhaps John would appear. After all, I was not exactly sure what I had experienced. Nor the parameters in which the experience was governed.

Perhaps John was my guardian angel of sorts and strumming the guitar summoned his presence. Much like a genie and having to rub its lamp to summon it. Or perhaps it was all a hallucination. Either way, playing the guitar sort of took my mind off it. I found myself focused on the music rather than if John appeared or not.

It was then, in that notion when the most peculiar thing occurred. The door to the acoustic room opened. Momentarily my emotion ran high with excitement as my strumming came to an abrupt halt. I thought for sure John had returned proving that what I experienced yesterday did in fact occur. That excitement was short lived. For it was not John that had come through the door. Instead, it was a tall slender African American young man.

He had hair that resembled the mane of a lion that spilled from beneath his wide brim western cowboy hat. The hat was peculiar indeed. Perhaps even a bit flamboyant for the times. It had a narrow purple band wrapped around it which was accompanied by various broaches and a rather large white feather.

The rest of his ensemble was just as much flamboyant. His jacket looked like something he had picked up at a British swap meet. It must have been wool in material maroon in color and was covered in polka dots of various sizes and colors. The shirt beneath the jacket surprisingly pulled it all together. It looked as if it was made of feathers. His pants black leather bell bottoms.

Though the young man seemed as if he had just walked in from 1970 there was something very admirable about him. Though admirable he was the fact was he was not who I was expecting. So, I went back to my strumming. I was playing working class hero. The song John had taught me the day before. The song caught the young man's attention stimulating him to comment.

"Oh, I know that... working class hero right," the young man asked wearing a smile that could light up a blackhole. "Just a second there let me join in with you," He went on as he grabbed a twelve-string guitar from the wall.

He pulled up a stool across from me and joined in. The two of us played the song in unison like a couple of rock legends. By the end of the song it was as if we had known one another our entire lives.

"Right on that was groovy," the Young Man said excitedly. "I'm Jimi, he went on as he extended his hand to me.

Unhesitant my hand met with his,

"I'm Michael," I replied.

"Well Michael you handle yourself quite well with that guitar," Jimi said complementing.

"Thanks... I'm still pretty novice," I explained.

"Novice... well you sure don't play like a novice," Jimi suggested. "How long have you been playing," Jimi went on to ask?

"Well that's the funny thing.... Today is my second day," I explained modestly.

"Far out your second day... Well isn't that something," Jimi marveled! "So how did you learn to play so well so fast," Jimi went on to asked?

My first instinct was to tell him about my experience with John. However, I was enjoying his company and did not want to scare him off. So, I made something up on the fly.

"Well I think it's just a deep desire to want to play and that gives me the stamina to keep playing for long periods, I explained. A friend of mine gave me a few pointers to help curb the learning," I went on.

"Well... it sure has paid off," Jimi said as he began to strum out a song. "Tell me what you think of this," he went on to suggest as he began to sing "Hear My Train Comin".

It was then in that moment I began to realize that something magical was occurring right before my eyes once more. Though I did not know much of Jimi Hendrix I had begun to believe that this young man was in fact him. It all began to make sense. The clothes, the hat, the guitar playing, the singing. It all added up.

As he played, I listened in marvel. It was then in the back of my mind I started to contemplate what really was happening to me. How was this possible? For the second day in a row I had come to the Guitar Shop and was visited and entertained by two deceased musical legends. Was I completely losing my mind? As I began to linger in that thought Jimi came to the end of his song.

"Well so... What do you think about that," Jimi asked optimistically?

"That was amazing Jimi... absolutely amazing," I suggested.

Apart of me wanted to address the fact that he was Jimi Hendrix. However, I was not sure what would happen if I did. So, I refrained. I mean though I was quite certain in my mind that he was Jimi Hendrix, I was not sure that my mind was in its right state. After all, only a couple of days prior I was locked in a mental hospital and I did not want to end up back there.

"Well here now you take this here twelve string and I will take that one and let's see you give that jam a try," Jimi suggested as he handed me the twelve string.

"Oh wow... you want me to play that number you just played," I asked as we swapped guitars.

"Yeah go ahead and give it a shot you saw the chords and hear the lyrics," Jimi insisted.

I would be lying if I said there was no doubt in the back of my mind. However, I figured what did I have to lose. I mean I was jamming out with Jimi Hendrix. So, I figured even the impossible was possible. I did see the chords he had played and for some reason though only hearing those lyrics for the first time I felt as if I knew them.

I began to strum the chords with great optimism. Then just as with John something took over. I let go and the song sort of played itself. I strummed the chords with precision not missing a note or a key. My vocals were just as crisp and pristine. By the end of the song, Jimi was my number one fan.

"Alright man now that was something else," Jimi said wearing a proud grin. "You are a natural," He went on.

I felt exhilarated. More confident than I had ever felt in my entire life. Hell, I felt alive for the first time in a long time. Perhaps even for the first time ever. Whatever was occurring in my life, I was happy it was. Even if it was all just a delusion in my own mind.

"Okay now I want you to check out this number," Jimi said as he reached down and plugged in the Gibson J-160E.

As he adjusted the levels to his desired tuning I waited in anticipation. When he started playing, "Hey Joe" there was no doubt in my mind that he was in fact the Jimi Hendrix. As I listened to Jimi play, I slipped into a trans like state. I began to pounder what it was I was experiencing. How was it possible that I had now met and jammed out with two deceased musical legends?

I wondered was I somehow seeing ghosts? Were my medications not working properly? Were these experiences nothing more than mere delusions despite how real they felt? Or perhaps it was not me at all. Perhaps it was the Guitar Shop that was somehow magical? Even that idea could be classified as delusional.

My mind raced with ideas trying to make sense of it all. Unfortunately, no rational concept came to mind.

Though the experiences were truly wonderful on some sense they were also a disturbance. Which led me to believe perhaps I needed to consult my therapist.

By the time Jimi made it to the end of the song I was overwhelmed by it all. I excused myself from the occurrence. I frantically stood to my feet stormed out of the Acoustic room like a bat out of hell making a bee line for the exit. I did not even say goodbye to Jimi. But as I pulled out of the parking lot in just as much of a frantic mess, I saw him standing in front of the Guitar shop smoking a cigarette in my rearview mirror.

My heart raced as anxiety took its toll. I was not exactly sure why I was having the anxiety attack. I mean I knew that it was valid response to what I experienced. However, being honest about it, it was the best thing that ever happened to me. A part of me felt as if I should have been jumping for joy rather running.

I guess the meds were working. Or at least attempting to. In that notion, as I did 70 mph all the way home barreling through all traffic lights, I decided to give Vivian a call. As the phone rang, I rehearsed what I would say. However, when she finally picked up none of what I rehearsed came out. Instead, a frantic mess was in its place.

"Hello this is Vivian," She answered.

"Doc I'm having a melt down here.... I mean I am seeing things that I shouldn't be seeing," I hyperactively blurted out! "I don't know what's real I don't know what's fake.... I mean what's happening to me," I frantically continued!

"Well first off you need to calm down everything is going to be okay," Vivian replied in a calming tone. "Now who am I speaking with," she went on?

"It's me... Michael... You know, we met the other day.... Um Michal Kingston," I managed to get out as I pulled into my driveway.

The car came to a sliding halt as I slammed on the brakes causing it to go from a 45 mph turn into the driveway to a stuttering stop.

"Okay Michael... Like I said, just try to calm down and articulately tell me what is going on," Vivian suggested. "Take a moment to gather yourself... everything is fine," she continued.

Deep down I knew she was right. I figured I must have been having a reaction to the meds. I took a deep breath, gathered myself and began to feel better. There was a momentary silence between us as I attempted to articulate mentally how to explain what I was experiencing. There was no rational explanation. I knew that. So, I told her precisely.

"Okay Vivian... So, I went to the guitar shop as you suggested to look for a guitar," I explained.

"Okay... and did something happen at the guitar shop that set you of Michael," Vivian consulted?

"Well, actually yes... you see while I was there the first day, I met John Lennon," I explained. "You know... the John Lennon... Sir John Lennon." I continued getting a bit razed again.

"Okay... just relax Michael," Vivian suggested.

"Relax... did you not hear what I just said," I asked accompanied by a sarcastic snicker. "I said I met John Lennon," I reiterated in an animated tone.

"Yes, I heard you just fine Michael," Vivian assured. "Though, my question for you is... what make you think you met Sir John Lennon," Vivian went on to ask calmly?

"Well, how about the fact that I jammed out with him... we shared small talk... and... and... he sang several of his songs right before my eyes," I suggested still quite revved up. "Not to mention, when we left... his famous Rolls Royce was in the parking lot.... He even taught me how to play "Working Class Hero"," I continued. "So, I know it was John Lennon," I went on.

"Hmmm... I see," Vivian gestured. "Well as bizarre as it may sound perhaps you did somehow meet Sir John Lennon," Vivian suggested.

"Excuse me," I rebutted taken by her response.

"Yeah, maybe you did meet John," Vivian reiterated. "I mean anomalies such as this happen all the time... who am I to say you were not the recipient of one,"

Vivian explained. "Now even still why do you feel such an occurrence has set you off," Vivian went on to ask?

"Well, I guess... I felt as though... I shouldn't be experiencing things like that," I explained.

"I see... and why do you feel you shouldn't be experiencing things like that Michael," Vivian asked?

"Well... it's like you said kind of bizarre... strange even," I replied in a shameful tone. "I mean... I just want to be normal and meeting Sir John Lennon doesn't constitute as normal right," I suggested?

"Well Michael, normal is a very fluid concept... especially when dealing with a condition such as yours," Vivian counseled. "The main thing you want to focus on is staying calm... you know, try not to get so worked up by these things," Vivian went on.

"So... you mean I can expect to have more occurrences like this and that's fine," I asked? "It's like part of my condition or something like that," I went on?

'Well not exactly, you see it's too early to say for sure what to expect being totally honest," Vivian consulted. "We have to give it some time and see what transpires with it all," She went on. "Perhaps you should take a break from guitar shopping for a couple days... get some rest and see how you feel then," Vivian suggested.

"Well... yeah I guess that's not a bad idea," I agreed.

"Well, unfortunately Michael that's all the time I have to spare today I have a client waiting to come in I do apologize," Vivian explained. "Do take it easy however and I will see you at our upcoming appointment," Vivian said on a closing note.

"Okay... will do and thank you so much doc for taking my call and helping me through this.... I really appreciate it," I replied before ending the call.

After speaking with Vivian despite feeling better I did not feel as though I got the answers I wanted. I mean, she basically told me that it was a 50/50 chance I was hallucinating versus meeting Sir John Lennon. Not to mention I did not even bring up meeting Jimi which in my mind was a validation that what I was experiencing was real. However, there was the slim possibility that it was not me at all and in fact has been the Guitar Shop all along. With that in mind I owed it to myself either eliminate or validate the possibility.

After a restless night, the next morning I skipped my morning ritual and decided to head straight out. Only this time I figured I would go to a different Guitar Shop to see if any mysterious event occurred. I figured if one did, then that would mean it was me that had the peculiar haunting. However, if it did not then it meant it was the Guitar Shop. I was more than desperate to get to the bottom off it all.

It really did not matter what Guitar Shop I went to if it was not the one in question. So, I just picked the next closest to my house which was Harvey's Guitars & More. When I pulled up to the place nothing seemed out of the ordinary. There were only a few cars in the parking lot which meant that Harvey's was not as popular as The Guitar Shop.

I pondered why this was so as I made my way to the entrance. Upon entry, my curiosity was answered. The place was a shabby old shack. In fact, it looked much better on the outside than inside. To top it off, there was no warm welcome like I received from Max. Instead, just a frail old man sitting behind a counter crammed in the back corner of the store.

The counter was tall and coupled with the cash register hid the old man who would have otherwise gone unnoticed had not he yelped out from behind.

"Welcome to Harvey's.... let me know if I can point you in the direction of anything," a raspy rickety voice called out. The voice sounded like death. Perhaps from lung cancer which would explain the pungent stale cigar smoke residue smell that infested the place. In fact, it was so pungent it gave my throat a tickle. More like irritated it.

Based off those facts I decided to leave the old man behind and give the place a gander all on my lonesome.

"No worries old timer... don't trouble yourself... I believe I can make my way around the place," I called out. "Heck if you been in one guitar shop you been in them all," I continued in a choky tone.

"Alright then suit yourself... I'll be here if you need me," the old man called out.

I assumed he was Harvey considering that he and the establishment look as if they belonged together. A bit of a duo of sorts. So, in response I called out.

"No worries Old man Harvey."

When he did not object, I took it as my assumption was correct and he was in fact Harvey. The thought of it gave me a bit of a chuckle as I proceeded to explore the place. After a brief peripheral observation of the small place I quickly realized there was no designated acoustic room. Just a few mediocre guitars hanging from the walls and a couple of stragglers picking the occasional one up for a strum. Despite this I figured the place would suffice for what I was trying to accomplish. So, I too picked a guitar from the wall took a seat and started to give it a strum.

Hours must have passed by without me realizing. It was not until old man Harvey called out his closing call that my attention was pulled from playing.

"Ten minutes to close folks," Harvey yelped.

When I looked up, I noticed I was the only one in the shop and had been for quite a while. I also noticed that the entire time I was there nothing out of the ordinary occurred. In fact, I was now convinced of one of two things. First, that there was a strong possibility that there was something magical about The Guitar Shop. Second, that if not I must have been having a weird allergic reaction to the meds. I was hoping the later.

That evening when I drove home my mind was bombarded with curiosity. I was under the impression that I might have stumbled upon something truly spectacular. Like a secret portal of sorts. I mean can you imagine. I could not wait to explore things further. I felt the giddiness of a child. That night I slept more peaceful than I had in a long time.

Chapter 4

Consultation

The next morning, I was more than eager to test the validity of my hypothesis. So, despite Vivian's advice I once again skipped my normal morning routine and headed straight out for the Guitar Shop. I was so excited I did not realize that I had left the house a bit early. I arrived at the Guitar shop about thirty minutes before they opened.

With the extra time on my hand I figured it was an opportune moment to rest my eyes a bit. Not necessarily meditate but drift deep in to thought. I contemplated if John or Jimi would show up and what the extremity of their presence would mean. I sure hoped one of them showed. It would at least assure me that I had not gone completely out of my mind just yet.

While deep in thought I must have nodded off. I was awakened by a knock on my passenger side window. A bit startled but aware I immediately saw a modest built African American staring in at me through the window. His voice was a bit muted by the glass, but I was able to make out what he said.

"Hey Partner, you alright in there," the young man asked through the window before knocking again as if he was not sure I had regained full conscious awareness? "It's too hot out here for you to be sleeping in there with the windows all rolled up," He went on.

I forced myself to pull it together and reached over to roll down the window before addressing the young man.

"Oh yeah I know... I must have dozed off waiting on the Shop to open but thank you I appreciate your concern," I explained.

"Well the Shop is open partner and have been here for a couple hours by my time," the young man said as he looked at his watch to verify the time.

"Oh really, geez that mean I have been out for a couple hours... again thanks I really do appreciate you," I said,

"Um hu... you sure you alright man... I mean you out here sleeping in your car in this scorching heat and caring on and your all disoriented," the young man asked in a concerned tone? "I mean do you need me to call like a paramedic or something," he went on to ask?

"Oh no... seriously I am fine... I'm actually getting out now and heading into the shop to get a guitar," I explained as I proceeded to get out of the car.

As I exited the car the young man double timed around to me and assisted with opening the door.

"Here let me help you with that," He said as he pulled the door open for me and reached his hand out to help me out of the car.

"Oh, thank you but really I'm fine," I said declining his assistance out of the car.

Despite my decline the young man just would not take no for an answer. Instead as I stood from the car, he took hold to my arm and held me steady. Honestly, I am glad he did because once to my feet I realized my legs were a bit wobbly. I guess I was starting to get heat exhaustion from the heat accumulated in the car from the sun.

"Well now partner I got you," the young man said as held me up. "So, you say you looking for a guitar," He went on as he held me while I regained the strength in my legs.

"Yeah that's right," I replied.

The young man chuckled at the idea.

"Well what's so funny about that," I asked now able to stand on my own.

"It's just... you don't look like much of a guitar player," The young man said as he took a step back to let me self-adjust.

His brutal honesty gave me a laugh. He was right I did not look like much of a guitar player. Heck I was not much of one for that matter. I mean other than the few licks I had learned for John and Jimi I was not a guitar player at all.

"Well, I guess I am aspiring," I explained that stimulated a good laugh for the both of us.

"I guess I can appreciate that," the young man replied. "The names Chuck," he went on as he extended his hand out for an official introduction.

"Well the pleasures all mine Chuck... Michael's the name," I said as I reciprocated to his gesture.

"Just so happen I'm looking for a guitar myself," Chuck said. "You know what... why don't we check a few out together," Chuck went on. "What the heck I'll show you a few things on the guitar while we're at it," He continued.

His offer did not sound like a bad idea. However, I did not know how him being in the equation would affect the probability of John or Jimi showing up. Then on the other hand, I figured if he were with me and one did show up, he would be a witness to the occasion and perhaps just as blown away as myself. With that in mind, I took him up on his offer.

"Yeah I think I would like that," I said as Chuck and I headed towards the entrance of the Guitar Shop.

Once in the shop there was Max just as chipper as ever.

"Welcome to the Guitar Shop home of the best selection around," Max called out while wearing a big smile. "Nice to see you again Michael is today the day," He went on to ask?

"Well... we shall see," I replied in a modest tone. "I will say one thing however, I am narrowing the search down, so we are getting close... I can feel it," I went on to explain.

"Nice... I'm glad you feel that way," Max said. "I know you are going to make a great player one day... I can feel it in my bones," He went on.

"I sure hope so," I replied.

"Alright then... I know you like to shop alone but just remember I am always here if you need me," Max reminded me.

"Indeed," I concurred as we parted ways.

Chuck and I then made our way to the acoustic room. Once in Chuck wasted no time. He went straight to a vintage 1950's Epiphone ES – 335 grabbed it from the wall and proceeded to rip through a riff that no one other than the late and great Chuck Berry could pull off. In that moment I knew, I was once again experiencing something magical.

My eyes now illumed with marvel and just about popping out of my skull. My mind was being stretched as if it was being pulled through a time warp. I could not believe my eyes nor my ears. I did not dare to confront the moment out of fear of losing it. So, I just smiled let of a slight chuckle of relief and nodded my head yes.

Chuck seemed to pay me no mind. He just ripped through riffs that seemed to capture my undivided attention. As he played them, I felt as if somehow, they were being programed into my psyche. Or even deeper, they were already there. It was in that moment something took over. If I had to explain it, I would describe it as perhaps muscle memory.

I picked up a Gibson Les Paul Standard from the wall plugged it in and began to rip through the same riffs Chuck was playing. He looked at me and smiled. It was then I began to formulate an idea of what I was experiencing. I was beginning to remember that which had been veiled for so long. I started to see vague glimpses of my fate. What I was born to do.

Chuck and I jammed out for hours. The time flew by and felt as if only seconds had passed. It was not until Chuck interrupted with the suggestion to play a song, he wanted me to learn that our downstream focus was interrupted.

'Alright now partner you getting the hang of this pretty quick," Chuck suggested. "I tell you what let me show you this song really quick... you will appreciate this number," He continued then went right into the riff of Johnny B. Goode.

As he played that riff the little doubt, I had of him being Chuck Berry was eradicated. Then when he dynamically burst into the lyrics to the song my jaw dropped to the floor. It was one of the most amazing things I had ever witnessed. In fact, I would rank it close to the birth of my children. By the end of the song, Chuck Berry had a new number one fan.

"Alright now what you think about that," Chuck asked wearing a satisfied grin?

"Well Chuck to be very honest, I'm in awe man... bravo," I replied then began to clap and bow to his genius.

Chuck burst into a frivolous laugh as he rehung the guitar to the wall. Then he turned to me and said his goodbyes.

"Alright now partner it's been a blast, but I better be getting on now," Chuck said now grinning ear to ear. "You take what we did here today and put it in your toolbox of tricks you hear me," he went on.

"Oh yes... most definitely I will do just that," I assured.

Then Chuck came over to me and pulled me in for a big hug. I did not know how to respond so rather than reciprocate I let him lead. I found myself clutched in his embrace with the only thing between us being the Gibson that I was still holding. After the hug Chuck just turned away and walked off. I did not follow him despite the urge. Instead, I sat back down and consciously played Johnny B. Goode.

While I played, I could feel my soul smiling. It was pleased for the first time in a long time. As was I. After the song I decided to head home. On the short drive home, I could not get what I had stumbled into off my mind. It would be an understatement to say I was blown away.

The recent occurrences I found myself experiencing were so profound a part of me needed to validate them by having someone other than myself experience it. So, I decided to give Jill a call. I could hear it in her tone when she answered the phone, she was not thrilled to be getting a call from me.

"What do you want Michael," Jill barked out from the other end of the phone?

"Well hey Jill," I replied politely attempting to defuse any tension she was harboring towards me.

"Michael... can I help you with something," Jill asked?

"Well actually Jill that's the thing... yes you can help me with something," I said. "You see, I've been going to see a counselor you know... to try to figure things out and get back on track," I went on. "Well, in one of our session she suggested I buy a guitar and give it a try to keep me occupied or something like that," I continued then paused briefly hesitant and now having doubts of whether I should tell Jill what I was about to.

"And Michael," Jill said in a tone that insisted she wanted me to get on with it already.

"So, I went to this Guitar Shop you know the one up the road where I sold my guitar... I figured maybe by chance they would still have it of course they didn't but that's beside the point," I explained. "Well, instead of finding my guitar I found something even more spectacular... you probably won't believe it unless you witness it yourself but there is some sort of time portal there that allows me to meet passed on rock legends," I proclaimed boldly.

As I waited on Jill's response the dead air that filled the line hinted that she was taken by what I had just laid on her. I began feeling the necessity to attempt to try and make her grasp what I had just shared despite knowing it was a bit farfetched. Who am I kidding perhaps it even gave her the impression that neither counseling nor the meds prescribed were working? I decided to try and smooth the blow of my revelation with reassurance.

"I know what you are thinking... I am out of my mind right," I suggested. "I thought the same thing at first until my therapist insisted that perhaps what I was experiencing was real," I went on. "That's when I decided to test the validity of the situation myself... So, I went to a different guitar shop to see if I witnessed anything out of the ordinary and I did not," I continued now a bit razed up. Then I went back to the Guitar Shop my Guitar Shop and it happened again," I explained.

"Um Michael... sweetheart let me cut you off right there... Hun I think you need to have your counselor up your dose and if she disagrees perhaps you need to find a new counselor," Jill arrogantly suggested.

"Jill... I thought the same thing and that was going to be my course of action until it happened again," I explained. "That's why I am now reaching out to you... I want you to come there with me and see for yourself," I went on. "When it happens then you will know what I am saying is real," I made out before Jill interrupted me.

"Michael, I tell you what... I will go to this Guitar Shop with you to prove you and your counselor are out of you minds and when I do babe we are going to get you some real help okay," Jill said before ending the call.

I could tell she was not pleased with the whole ordeal. However, I knew that once she saw for herself things would be different. I wanted to make sure that she was able to experience it for herself so I decided that we should go when the guitar shop opened as I had done the previous times it occurred. Considering she ended the call so abruptly I decided to text her the time and location to meet up.

I did not sleep a lick that night. I was anxious about how things would unfold. So, by the time morning had arrived I was both anxious and exhausted. However, that was not going to stop me. I was determined to prove not only to Jill but to myself as well that what I experienced was real.

When I arrived at the Guitar Shop Jill was already there waiting in her car. I pulled into the spot next to her and quickly exited my car to greet her.

"Good morning Jill," I said as I made my way to open her door for her. "I really appreciate you coming and mark my words you are going to be blown away," I continued as she exited her car.

Once she was out of her car, I tried to give her a friendly hug, but it just morphed into an awkward shuffle of sorts. Trying not to make thing any more awkward than they already were I quickly transitioned to leading the way to the door.

"Okay... my apologies for that," I said referring to the hug as we made our way to the entrance of the Guitar Shop. "Allow me," I went on as I reached out to open the door for Jill.

Upon entry there was Max with his friendly welcoming smile.

"Morning Michael," he greeted as Jill and I entered. "I see you have brought a second set of eyes with you today," He went on.

Briefly I found him acknowledging Jill rather peculiar considering he had never acknowledged anyone else with me prior. I am sure he must have seen me with Chuck because the two of us entered the store together as Jill and I had. Perhaps he even saw me leave with John or jam out with Jimi. After all it all had taken place in his presence. Or at least I thought. Perhaps, I was wrong altogether.

Though I was disturbed by the notion of it I forced it to the back of my mind determined to accomplish what I set out to.

"Well I reckon it's always nice to have a second set of eyes," I said to address Max statement.

Then Jill and I continued and made our way right past Max. We did not stop until we were standing before the acoustic room. It was there before entering I took a moment to gather myself. I closed my eyes and took a deep breath while saying a silent prayer mentally to aid my ambition then proceeded to pull the door open.

As always, I was greeted by that glorious smell of fresh oaks and pines. The sight of the guitars even seemed to amaze Jill which was not always an easy task. I saw the excitement in her eyes, and it brought a smile to my face. She resembled a kid in a candy store. It was a charming encounter.

She wasted no time with making herself acquainted with the instruments. First, she strummed a few while they were still hanging on the wall. Then surprisingly she grabbed one from the wall took a seat on a nearby stool and started trying to familiarize herself with the fret board. I figured since no one had arrived I would join along and try to show her a few things that I had learned so far.

I picked up my usual one from the wall and proceeded to show her a few things. She was thrilled by my knowledge. I was thrilled by her interest in listening to me. It was a rare occurrence for sure. The two of us had not gotten along or had as much fun together since we had first met. It reminded me of the thing I really liked about her and I imagine vice versa.

It was the first time in a long time that I had seen Jill without the presence of the wall that over the years formulated and stood between us. The two of us had so much fun we lost track of time and hours had went by before we realized it. It was Jill who first realized due to having to be home to receive the kids from school and daycare.

"Oh, Michael it is already 2:45 P.M. you know I have to pick up Bethany from daycare and be home to get Riley off the school bus," Jill said.

I knew this to be the case therefore I did not object. I could also see it in her eyes that she was trying to be compassionate by not mentioning how no one showed up. Instead she surprised me with her next suggestion.

"You know what Michael why you don't come with me... I am sure the kids would be happy to see you," Jill went on.

Though I was disappointed and confused the idea of spending time with Jill and the kids lightened the blow. Honestly, it did more than lighten the blow. It defused what may have turned into a manic episode. Perhaps even prevented me from serving another stint at Memorial Behavioral. The idea of it all inspired me to sing a song.

"Okay Jill... I think that would be a good idea," I agreed. "Hey, you know what but before we go let me sing you a song," I went on to suggest as Jill stood to leave.

Jill seemed surprised by the suggestion because she had never really heard me play an actual song. In fact, I do not even think she believed I could. So, her reaction to the suggestion did not surprise me. I took her hand and sat her back down then I looked her in her eyes and started to play.

I honestly do not know where the song came from because prior to that day I had not heard it. The song was "To Fall in Love With You" by Bob Dylan. By the end of the song, I had a new number one fan. When I looked upon Jill after the song, she was in tears but smiling. Before I could say anything, Jill had thrown herself into my arms. Then she softly whispered in my ear.

"I have always loved you Michael."

Her words left me speechless because I knew I had reached Jill. Probably for the first time in all the time I had known her. She saw me for who I was, and I saw her. I could feel it. We left the Guitar Shop that day closer than we had ever been. That night when it was all said and done, we sat down as a family and had dinner together for the first time since the separation.

Chapter 5

Reconciliation

The next morning, I was awakened by a distant but familiar sound. It took me a moment to gain full composure but when I did the sound was accompanied by familiar surroundings. I found myself in Jills bed listening to the once accustomed morning commotions as her and the kids got ready for the day. I laid there and lingered in the familiarity. It was soothing.

It was not until Jill popped her head into the door and saw that I was awake that I was pulled from that moment.

"Michael... good morning love," Jill said as she slid into the room and shut and locked the door behind her. "So, about last night...," She went on as she made her way over to the bed and took a seat next to me. "I don't want the girls to get the wrong idea about things... I mean... I am glad about whatever this is and whatever it means but until we know exactly what that is let us hide it from the girls... okay," Jill explained.

"Yes... I guess I agree that makes sense," I agreed.

Being completely honest in that moment I could not believe how I ever let her slip out of my life. She sat there before me so elegantly as her beauty vibrantly radiated from her. As I stared off into her eyes, I wanted nothing more than to stay there in that moment with her. In that moment where our petty differences that tore us apart seemed nonexistent.

"Okay love... so just stay in here until I get the girls off then I will be back to talk with you if that is okay with you," Jill suggested.

"Yes of course, I would like that," I was able to make out before Jill planted a surprising kiss to my lips then jumped out of bed and darted for the door.

"Girls you better be brushing your teeth," I heard her yell out as the bedroom door closed behind her.

I must admit though I was taken and left in a trans by her absolute beauty a part of me was anxious about what had occurred last night between the two of us. I wondered what it meant. I also based my impression of it based off what she had just shared. Jill was still very much in love with me and wanted our family to be together.

Despite wanting the same I knew it would mean I would have to conform to her views of things. I also knew that it would mean I would have to give up on exploring the guitar shop further. Perhaps even dismiss the one person that for once kind of sort of got me and all my quirks, Vivian. It was then, in that notion I realized I was not sure I was going to be able to live up to her expectations.

My mind formulated from beginning to end the various scenarios that could unfold. One seemed to justify the pursuit of whatever it was Jill wanted between us. So, it was all I needed to convince myself that if the opportunity was presented to accept Jill's invitation of love. Who was I kidding, I was more than eager to do so?

After she had gotten the kids off to school and returned, she entered the bedroom once more. I was still there where she had left me entranced by my own thoughts. It was her voice that pulled me from them.

"So, Michael my love... as you know I am deeply in love with you and always have been," She proclaimed as she made her way towards me. "I will always love you and want nothing more than to be with you and for you to be here where you belong with us... your family," She went on now standing before me.

I looked up into her eyes and saw her sincerity. She then placed herself straddled my lap facing me and wrapped her arms around my neck resting them on my shoulders. Her fingers caressed through the hair of the back of my head sending a chilled sensation down my back. Silence filled the room as we gazed into each other's eyes.

I patiently awaited her next words hoping they would continue in the direction they were headed. Then they came catching me by surprise even though deep down I expected them to arrive.

"Though I love you... I have reservations," Jill said in a disconcerting tone. "This new fixation of yours with this guitar shop and seeing deceased rock stars is a bit much," She explained. "I mean... for us to work you will have to promise me that you are done with that," Jill continued.

The room once more filled with silence. Jill now awaited my response. I knew what I needed to say and deep down I knew I could say it. However, I was not sure that I would be able to live up to my words. The

Guitar Shop was not just a fixation to me as Jill had deemed it. For me, I strongly felt it was my destiny.

Despite having my own reservation, I wanted to be with Jill and the girls. So, against my better judgement I made a commitment I only hoped I would somehow live up to.

"Jill... my love, all that is behind me if it means I will have you," I proclaimed convincingly.

So convincingly I even managed to convince myself. Another rare trait of mine I had grown fond of. The ability to sell myself on things even when the chances of them coming into fruition were slim. Well, perhaps even that was the case with the Guitar Shop. You see, that was the thing. I did not know for sure and it would haunt me if I did not see it through.

I mean really, what good would I be to Jill or the girls with something like that eating away at my conscious. This was the convincing factor I use to sell myself on the idea to secretly see the Guitar situation out. I figured if I played my cards right there was a winning scenario for us all. At least I liked to believe so.

As I stared into Jill's eyes that morning, I could see deep down she wanted to believe me. Hell, I even wanted to believe me. So, we both did just that. For the most part any way. At least, I was able to sell myself on that idea. Only time would truly tell whether I was correct or not.

The room was silent after my proclamation to cease pursuit of the Guitar Shop mystery. We both lingered in the possibilities of what that meant. It was a very heartwarming moment. Personally, I still had that buzz I often got after a blissful night with Jill. I could also see that buzz lingering in her eyes.

The craving for more was mutual. Therefore, with the kids out of the house and the two of us officially committing to giving things another shot, we celebrated with a consummation. The experience was like no other we had ever shared. Much more than a connection of vanity. Much more than mere a consummation of the flesh.

Surprisingly, things seamlessly fell into a familiar routine with Jill in the girls. The first few days went by in an all-consuming manner. We were all consumed by one another. It was sheer bliss. Not once did I think of the Guitar Shop.

The days turned into weeks. Then the weeks turned into the first month milestone of our reconciliation. It had been awhile since I had last saw Vivian. Jill thought it was best to decrease the frequency of our visits given she was a supporter of the Guitar Shop venture.

Then, out of nowhere a scheduled visit had emerged. It had completely slipped my mind. It was Jill who had brought it to my attention. Given the gesture, I assumed we had developed a level of trust over the weeks. Jill now trusted that the Guitar Shop business was behind us. As did I.

That morning started like every other as Jill spooned me from behind. It was her hand that slowly made its way around to my chest then down past my belly not stopping until it found its way into my briefs that captured my waking attention. Then when that hand gently contacted my member it stimulated my awareness. Her warm breath scaling down my neck prior her lips contacting it. Then those words that will never cease to stimulate a smile throughout my entire body.

"Good Morning handsome," Jill whispers sending chills throughout my body. "Oh my, someone is excited to hear my voice," she went on giving notice to my member stiffening in her hand. "Well it is quite unfortunate that you are going to have to save that for later," Jill continued.

Her commentary caused me to have to force back my smile and giggles. Honestly, it was hard to accomplish because she was so freaking cute. I quickly rolled over to her unable to suppress my joy any longer and proceeded to mount her playfully.

"What do you mean save that until later," I called out in a playful tone as I smothered her with kisses and affection. "You know it is humanly impossible for me to resist you," I went on now kissing her breast through her shirt causing her to laugh hysterically.

"Michael I am being serious now," She was barely able to make out due to her laughter. "You have a big day my love," She went on as she pushed me off her.

I willingly allowed myself to be tossed from her and landed back into the bed with an airy plop on to my back.

"A big day you say my love," I called out in a renaissance accent. "And what might it be that will keep me so occupied that I do not have time to mount my lady, I continued now in a broken British accent.

"Well, for one it is your day to get the girls to school," Jill replied as she mounted me. "Then... you have to visit that therapist of yours," She went on as she ran her index fingernail from my throat down my chest stopping at my heart. "Despite I don't like her I feel like you continuing therapy is a good thing... so, for now until you find a new therapist you will see her," She continued. "This is not a problem is it," She went on to ask?

"No... these requests are flawless my love and I foresee no problems," I assured now back into my renascence accent.

Then as I smiled up at her she leaned in and kissed my lips. When she tried to end the kiss, I pulled her back in for more.

"I love you," I proclaimed when I finally let her from the grips of my seductive kisses.

"Awe... I love you too Michael," Jill reciprocated.

"Okay... now dismount me woman I have things to see and people to do or wait things to do and people to see," I said charmingly as I assisted Jill off me with a quick roll leaving me now on top of her.

For a moment, as I hovered over her and she griped my arms I took in her beauty.

"Okay now I can go about my day," I said as I stood to my feet. "And as for you... General, you will have to wait till later as my lady has advised," I addressed to the salute I adjusted in my briefs. "Girls... I hope you are awake and getting ready for school," I called out as I grabbed my robe from the hook on the bedroom door and headed out to start the day.

By this time, I was once again a master at the morning routine. Reclamation was a breeze. I had the girls and myself dressed in out the door within forty-five minutes. The less than fifteen-minute drive to their school aside from Riley voicing her opinion about us being a family once more was rather silent. Though she was only seven years old she possessed an ageless awareness.

"Dad... I am happy we are all a family again," Riley said in a compassionate tone.

"Me too sweetheart, I am happy we are all a family again as well," I assured her as we pulled into the school drop off zone.

Once the car came to a safe stop, I turned to her in the back seat. My beautiful Riley I thought to myself as she gathered her things and proceeded to exit the car.

"Riley...," I called out before she could shut the door.

"Yes dad," She responded.

"You know I love you right sweetheart," I told her in a sincere tone.

"Of course, dad, always and forever... I am your Sun and your Moon right," She said wearing a proud smile.

"That's right love... my Sun and my Moon," I replied now sharing her proud smile. "Have a good day sweetheart," I went on.

"You too dad," Riley said as she shut the door then made her way to her class line.

Since Bethany was in a toddler class, I had to pull around to the front of the school park and take her inside myself. I guess the teachers were against carrying car seats occupying fifteen plus pound toddlers from the drop off lane. Honestly, I cannot object because the thought of doing such a thing is so absurd. Can you imagine having to lug twenty plus toddlers fifteen plus pound toddlers in car seats to class. I had but mildly began to appreciate carrying my one toddler in.

Once to Bethany's class I noticed we were the first to arrive. I took it as an opportunity to have a word with her teacher, Mrs. Richardson. I gave her applaud and my praises for the job she does daily. I also thanked her for doing it in such a safe and efficient manner. Then, without further ado I was off to my adult tasks, therapy.

On the ride over to Vivian's office I contemplated how the session would go. I also contemplated how she would take the news of me deciding to go with a different therapist. Heck, I was not exactly sure how I was taking the news. Deep down I did not want to switch therapist. I mean, I was not ready to let go of the only person that accepted me truly as I was. From a therapeutic perspective it did not seem logical.

Good grief, the decisions a man must make. On one hand I have Jill who is insistent that I switch therapist and on the other I have my personal preference and desire. I mean Vivian was someone I was growing to value as a part of my support system. I was not prepared to let her go.

When I arrived, she was already in the lobby waiting on my arrival. We shared a short greeting then headed straight back to her office.

"Good morning Michael, Vivian called out.

"Morning Vivian," I replied as she turned to lead the way back.

As we made our way down the hall, I was wrestling with the different approaches I could take to break the news. None of which seemed sufficient given the value I had placed on Vivian's role in my life. Once in her office before I could address the elephant in the room Vivian did the unthinkable. From behind her desk she pulled out a guitar and gave it a brisk strum.

"So, Michael I had a thought the other night while contemplating what you have shared with me thus far," Vivian shared as she proceeded to tune the guitar.

"Given you have not had any formal guitar lessons and have only been searching to purchase a guitar for a couple weeks now so I imagine your playing skills will reflect that," She explained. "However, if for some reason you have been visited by the late and great Sir John Lennon and personally taught to play his song "Working Class Hero" then surely you should be able to play it now," She went on then extended the guitar out in effort to hand it to me.

Honestly at first, I did not know how to respond to the gesture. My first thought was how dare her put me on spot like this. I quickly went into my defensive mind and assumed she was attempting to judge me. I figured her actions had derived from a place of doubt. Briefly I stared at her and the guitar in a state of shock of sorts.

Then something took over me. That same something that had took over me in the Guitar Shop.

"Well I reckon you make a valid point," I said as I reached out a grabbed the guitar from her.

Once in my hands I quickly noticed the guitar was a Martin in new condition.

"Nice a Martin hey," I unconsciously blurted out as I began to tune the guitar. "GPC Special Koa X Series," I went on.

Vivian did not seem taken by my knowledge of the instrument instead she just watched and waited to see what would transpire.

"You almost had it tuned perfectly except that high -E need a little more twang for this particular song," I suggested then proceeded to test my tuning with a quick stroke of the strings.

"Perfect, I proclaimed before diving right into the song.

Though the song was only four minutes at best it felt like eternity. Even more so, I felt for the first time that playing the guitar and singing songs like "Working Class Hero" was what I wanted to do for eternity. I felt the words of that song radiating through me. I wanted to be a working-class hero. I somehow in that moment knew it was what I was supposed to be.

By the end of the song I was not the only one who felt this way. Vivian was left in complete marvel at my performance.

"Oh my... absolutely stunning Michael," Vivian suggested. "I have to say after hearing you play this song I am convinced," Vivian said. "Somehow you have been chosen and given this special gift," She went on. "A gift not only to play the guitar but also to miraculously congregate with rock n roll greatest musicians despite them already having passed on," Vivian said without reservation. "Now from a clinical standpoint I should not encourage this Michael however from an instinctual perspective I must encourage it," Vivian explained. "Michael, I am not sure how or why, but I believe you are experiencing a divine intervention and you must at all cost see this through," Vivian suggested boldly.

The room went silent momentarily. I could not believe my ears. Vivian had just given me the best and the worst information of my life. I knew that if she was convinced then what I was experiencing at the Guitar Shop was real. I also knew that her giving me the green light and encouraging it I would continue to pursue the Guitar Shop mystery despite Jill wanting it to seize.

This was a bit troubling for me because I did not want to lose Jill and the girls again. I knew that the continued pursuit of the Guitar Shop mystery very well could mean just that. However, despite the risk being as great as they were, I knew I had no choice in the matter.

Chapter 6

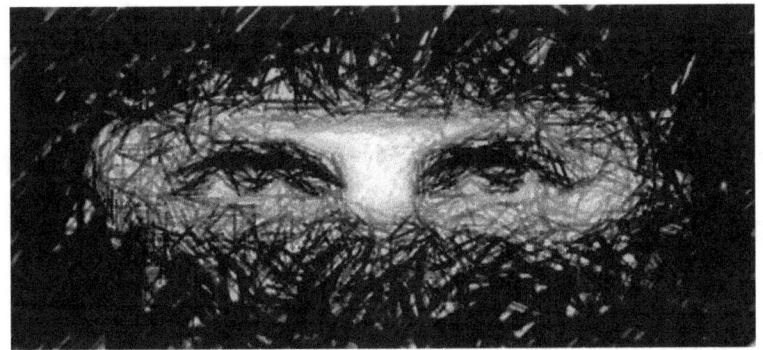

Liberation

I chose not to disclose the authentic outcome of my therapy session with Jill. Instead, I allowed her to assume I had followed through with her request to replace Vivian. I was able to sell the idea because I resisted the urge to go to the Guitar Shop for weeks following the session. Not to mention I had not had the need to make any emergency calls to Vivian.

Over the weeks Jill, myself, and the girls had readjusted to our normal flow of life. I was spending more and more time with Jill and the girls. So much time it was almost as if I lived there again. I kept my place and occasionally went there to decompress. It was during one of those decompress sessions when the irresistible urge took hold of me.

I found myself contemplating the events that I had experienced at the Guitar Shop. There was something undeniably captivating about them. I mean, I was being visited by deceased rock legends. Surely there must have been a reason for the encounters. A reason valid enough for me to unveil.

It was that notion that took hold of me that day. Then while heavily intoxicated and influenced by that notion I found myself once again standing in that Guitar Shop. Once again making my way across the long narrow strip to that acoustic room where all the magic had before time and again taken place. The only thing on my mind was who would I encounter.

I paid no regard to the time and actions in between mere contemplation and standing before the door to that acoustic room that day. Everything other than the mystery that laid before me was but a vague haze. My heart rate increased as I reached my hand out to take hold of the door handle to let myself into what I had come to acknowledge a paradise. I could feel something special brewing and only moments away.

As the door swung open, I was once again greeted by that smell I had grown to love so dearly. That smell represented liberation of sorts. My liberation from the mundane. After all it was this Guitar Shop acoustic room that had revitalized my hope. Revitalized my will to go on.

I optimistically walked into the room and stared down the wall of guitars once more. I slowly inhaled the smell of all the various woods and strings and peace and stillness were bestowed upon me. I closed my eyes and lingered in that bliss to savor the moment. When I finally opened my eyes, she practically jumped off the walls and into my arms.

She was a 1959 Martin D-18E. I called it a she because it was so sexy. Her lines displayed perfect curvature. Her stain was the perfect hue. Her neck finely elongated stretched upward and elegantly merged with her headstock.

She was a work of beauty and displayed fine craftmanship. The type of craftmanship that gave me the impression that her creator created her with a special woman in mind. The result was that fine instrument. So, out of respect it dawned on me that the 1959 Martin D-18E hanging on the wall that day was indeed she.

When I took her from the wall and held her in my hands it felt like a match made in heaven. I knew she was the one. Perhaps not the one I had been looking for but indeed the one I needed. The idea of it brought a heart-warming smile to my face. It was that smile that caught the attention of a patron as he entered the acoustic room,

"Well... it looks like you found you one and a nice one at that," He said as he entered the room catching my attention.

When I looked upon the man at first glance, I thought my eyes were playing tricks on me. I thought to myself could it be? Then I remembered where I was and was reassured my eyes were seeing correct. My eyes were indeed looking upon yet another rock legend.

He was a slim and bashful looking fellow. He must have stood about five foot nine or so. He had straggly blonde hair that could have been considered a bit long for a guy. His scruffy unkept face gave the impression that he really did not care about his appearance.

His rough and raged clothes told the same tale. His shoes over run Converse Chuck Taylors concurred. His entire ensemble represented his grunge attitude. Though the thing that stood out even more than all those tale - tale signs was his prominent butted chin. It was a dead giveaway of his identity.

His cold deep-sea blue eyes glared at me awaiting a response. I must admit I was speechless momentarily. I was still quite uncertain how to approach the situation considering. I mean I had witnessed now three different deceased rock legends all in which like myself seemed to have no clue what nor how we were experiencing what we were.

So, I decided it was best to just go with the flow and allow things to unfold organically. Without calling out the elephant in the room I managed to reciprocate words and still maintain my composure.

"Yeah... she is a beauty right," I asked attempting to stimulate a conversation.

"She sure is... you mind," he asked waiting to hold the work of art.

"Sure, brother be my guest," I said as I handed him the guitar. "I'm Michael by the way and you are," I asked anxiously waiting for my speculations to be validated.

"My name is Kurt but everyone one calls me Pixie Meat," he replied.

"Pixie Meat... that's an interesting nickname," I said.

"Yeah... I thought so too," Kurt said as he let off a chuckle.

"Well I hope you don't mind but how did you get a name like Pixie Meat," I asked despite knowing it was a name given to him by Kourtney Love because of his diminutive size and his bizarre worship like obsession with the Pixies.

"To be honest I am not quite sure," Kurt said still chuckling over the humorous nick name.

The idea of him not knowing how he got that nick name filled me with sympathy rather than sending up red flags about the authenticity of his identity. I sympathized with him out of the realization that he seemed to have no clue who he was. Was this because he was perhaps a pre-Nirvana Kurt? Or worse, like stuck in some Devachan purgatory for committing suicide.

Before I could drift too deep into thought Kurt began to play the guitar. The chords he strummed sounded very familiar. Then when he began to sing along to them the lyrics to "Heart Shaped Box" everything else seemed to lose importance. He had captured my devote attention. By the end of the song there was no doubt in my mind. He was the Kurt Cobain no matter if he knew it or not.

"Wow that was amazing," I said in a giddy tone.

"Yeah... thanks man glad you liked it," Kurt said bashfully accompanied with chuckles.

"So, have you been playing long," I asked?

"Honestly... feels like my whole life," Kurt said. "My aunt Mari and I used to sing a lot starting around two and then she got me on the piano when I was four," He went on. "The rest well... is still in the making I guess," Kurt explained.

"Wow... since you were two that's pretty impressive," I suggested. "I am just starting out myself," I continued.

"Well it is never too late to get started," Kurt said in an encouraging tone. "You know what they say... better late than never right," He continued.

"Yeah... I guess you are right," I agreed. "So, what do you plan on doing with all that talent," I went on to ask?

"Well... me in a couple of my buddies are starting a band," Kurt said. "We are calling ourselves Fecal Matter," He went on. "Of course, it is all preliminary currently, but it is off to a good start I guess," He continued.

"A band called Fecal Matter that is interesting," I suggested.

"Well it is just a name," Kurt said suggesting the name of the band was not important to him. "It is kind of a joke band to be honest," He continued.

"A joke band... what is a joke band," I asked?

"You know like not really having any real musical substance," Kurt explained. "However, we do have Dale from Melvins playing bass which is kind of cool," Kurt continued. So, we get a little bit of a following sort of a spin off from the Melvins," He went on.

"Nice... that sounds like a lot of fun," I suggested.

"Yeah it is fun I guess," Kurt said. "I mean... I like being in a band and all but perhaps not my current one," He went on.

"Is that so," I asked in a concerned tone?

"Yeah but don't get me wrong I appreciate the opportunity and have learned a lot from being in Fecal Matter, but I see myself being bigger than that," Kurt explained. "Besides, I don't think Fecal Matter will make it very far," He continued. "But my next band... Nirvana will be something special.

"Nirvana... now that sounds like a legendary band if I do say so myself," I said reassuringly hoping to encourage Kurt to pursue that dream.

"I know right... I sure think so," Kurt said. It is a Buddhist concept which I feel captures my true essence and aspirations," He went on. It means freedom from pain, suffering and the external world," Kurt continued.

"I really like that Kurt... it has substance for sure from the ideology standpoint and with your talent I do believe it will be something great," I said encouragingly.

"Thanks man... you know you are an alright guy," Kurt said. "Here... let me show you a few quick tricks on this guitar," He continued as he began to strum through a few chord progressions.

He had me. I was all ears. Learning more guitar tricks from the late and great Kurt Cobain himself. In the depth of his magical guitar lesson it dawned on me that there may have been a way to get the best of both worlds. My pursuit of the Guitar Shop and my family.

If I were able to prove to Jill that what I was experiencing was in fact real she would have no choice but to accept it. So, I decided to pull out my phone and use the voice memo to record Kurt and me. He had no clue of this, and I did not think he would mind nor need to know what I was doing. Instead, after pulling up the app and hitting record I put my phone back in my pocket and gave Kurt my undivided attention.

By the end of the lesson I felt like a well-rounded guitarist despite the lesson only being forty-five minutes or so. Teaching and singing must have aroused Kurt's appetite because his first suggestion after the last note strummed was to go to lunch.

"Oh man I sure could go for a bite to eat now," Kurt said. What do you have going on... you hungry," Kurt went on to ask?

"Actually, I do not have anything planned and could go for some lunch," I said agreeing to his suggestion to grab a bite to eat.

"Cool... well before we go, I think I am going to buy this guitar... I mean unless you had your heart set on it after all you did have it first," Kurt said voicing his interest in the beautiful guitar that had stolen my heart.

What was I to say to that? Who was I to deny Kurt that instrument? So, I did what I believe what anyone would have done and let him have it.

"Oh, if you want her brother, she is all yours," I assured. "Besides, I kind of am looking for a specific guitar," I continued referencing back to my search for the Guitar that had started it all.

I guess underneath all the mystical and metaphysical phenomenon I was temporarily distracted from my search for Apollo's guitar. However, it remained at the core of it all. Without the notion to search for it, who knows where I would be?

"Right on man," Kurt said expressing his gratitude for me allowing him to have the guitar. "To show my appreciation lunch on me today man, He continued.

I must be honest I was a bit taken by the idea of Kurt wanting to buy the guitar. I was not sure how that would work considering. Would he be able to? I mean, would the clerk see him? My mind raced with ideas as we made our way to the counter.

Once there Kurt simply handed the guitar over and the clerk rang him up like he would have any other customer. I stood there by Kurt's side in complete silence and watched the transaction. The experience was rather illusionary. Yet somehow very real.

After purchasing the guitar, we passed Max on our way out. He was still just as pleasant as ever.

"Have a nice day Michael and by the way nice selection," He called out as Kurt and me exited the Guitar Shop.

"Indeed," I said as the door closed behind us.

Once in the parking lot Kurt pulled out a pack of smokes. American Spirit Menthols was his smoke of choice. As he pulled one from the pack and lit it, we stood momentarily in front of the Guitar Shop. It was his voice that disrupted the brief silence that had formed between us.

"Well shall we," He said from behind a cloud of smoke he exhaled. "We have to go in your car because my roommate dropped me off here," He continued.

"Oh, sure brother no worries... I am right over there," I said pointing to my car across the parking lot.

As we made our way to the car Kurt shared more philosophy about his ideal band. Honestly if I did not know any better, I would have solicited joining said band. However, I did not think that was even possible, so I fought the urge to do so. The more time I spent with Kurt the more I pondered on his controversial death.

The Kurt I was experiencing that day did not seem like the type of guy that would want to take his own life. In fact, the Kurt I was experiencing that day did not seem like he could ever become the Kurt that supposedly took his own life. Made me wonder if there was more to the story than the world was introduced to.

I did not want to spoil lunch so on the drive to Chipotle I kept my ideas of conspiracy theory to myself. Besides, Kurt would not have even had a clue what I was talking about considering he had no idea about his life that I knew. So instead, we listened to music. He introduced me to a new artist he liked that went by the name Jose Gonzalez.

I was blown away by Jose's music and over the short drive to lunch I became a fan.

Once at Chipotle we ordered burritos took a seat and shared some ideas. Kurt mostly talked about how he was tired of High School. Knowing who he was I assured him that he would get much further in life saying the hell with high school and pursuing his dream. Kurt agreed it was time to start taking his career more seriously. He gave me the impression that I had gotten through to him.

After lunch I took him home and bid him fair well. Then I felt myself more than eager to show Jill the recording I had captured of Kurt and my session. I knew it was going to be the pinnacle point of our relationship. She would no longer be able to deny what I was experiencing at the Guitar shop. I could not wait to experience her reaction.

I drove straight to her place overly proud of my accomplishment. So proud of myself I did not even think to check the recording to make sure it was sufficient. That would soon prove to be the biggest downturn in events that day. Once I arrived at her place I stormed right through the door and called out for her.

"Jill," I yelled in an excited tone. "Honey you won't believe it, but I have proof," I went on as she made her way into the kitchen where I was.

"Michael what is the matter sweetheart is everything okay," Jill asked in a startled tone?

"Yes, my love everything is fine and when you hear this recording things will be even better, I proclaimed as I pulled up what I believed was the recording from earlier with Kurt.

"Hear what baby," Jill asked?

"The recording of me and Kurt Cobain at the Guitar shop," I blurted out prematurely without thinking of the repercussions of my words.

"The Guitar Shop... Michael are we seriously back here," Jill asked in a concerned tone?

"I know what you are thinking but before you say anything just listen, I said as I hit play on the recording.

The recording caught me by more of a surprise than Jill. What I thought was my proof that would liberate me from the possible delusion pool turned out to be my reckoning. At least from Jills perspective. The recording was a disaster. Somehow between pushing record and putting the phone back in my pocket something went wrong. All I had recorded was a bunch of white noise.

"What is this Michael... you promised," Jill said in a disappointed tone.

"But I do not understand... how is that possible," I said as I double checked the device to assure, I was not perhaps on the wrong recording.

Unfortunately, the recording I thought I had captured was nowhere to be found. I looked like a complete tool. The room filled with silence and tension. Jill was not very happy with me in that moment. In fact, she was furious.

I know she had a right to be mad. After all I was being a bit deceitful going to the guitar shop behind her back. However, even still I was not prepared for what she was about to pull.

"Michael...," her voice called out pulling me from my deep thought. "Enough is enough this has got to stop," she went on. "This is absolutely the last straw you either put this behind you or put me and the girls behind you," she boldly gave her final ultimatum.

It caught me by surprise. I really did not know how to answer. I knew after the day I experienced at the Guitar Shop I could not stop. I was on to something great. I had to see it through.

I also knew that I would no longer be able to leave Jill in the dark because now she would be expecting it. I felt as if I had no other choice in the matter. So, I did the noble thing and I walked out. I chose what I have come to believe was my fate.

Chapter 7

Determination

So once again there I was back at my whole in the wall apartment all alone, aside from my haunting thoughts that seemed to intentionally antagonize. Though I was not ready to let Jill and the girls go I was left with no other choice. Jill had put her foot down and with good reason. I was a jerk all things considered.

Despite that the first few days following the split I blamed Jill for being so harsh. My brief resentment towards her was short lived for I found other things to keep me occupied. There was the occasional trip to the corner pub where I would indulge in watered down booze and severely germ exposed peanuts until I had my due fill. What can I say I was trying to drown out my sorrows?

Then there was the ritualistic Salisbury steak tv dinner that I would eat in my recliner while watching reruns of Highway to Heaven until I passed out. Often this resulted in me dropping what I believe was mash potatoes onto the already stained 1970's psychedelic shag carpet. It and I had both seen better days. Then there were my visits with Vivian.

Vivian was still a strong supporter of me continuing my pursuit of the Guitar Shop Mysteries. She proclaimed it was the only way to finally see who or what I truly was. I believe therefore she was bothered by the fact I had put a halt to the endeavor despite already having paid the ultimate price to pursue it. You know, losing Jill and the girls and all. In the end, it was her bold confrontations that set me straight.

Six long isolating months had passed since I had last been to the Guitar Shop. I guess the inevitable was long overdue. It had been so long I did not know what to expect when I arrived. I thought perhaps the anomaly had dried up. It would have made things easier.

Despite that notion I longed for it to still be a part of my reality of sorts. I wanted what I had been experiencing to have deep resonating meaning. Even more so I wanted to comprehend and understand said meaning as it pertained to me and my life. At least that way I could set things straight with Jill.

As I approached the entrance and reached out to take hold of the door, I felt my heart flutter with excitement. I had a feeling something special was about to occur and was more than eager to experience it. Upon entry I noticed the place was unusually packed. A sense of anxiety came over me. I wondered had my secret got out and now the Guitar Shop was at the center of some spectacle?

I did not let this discourage me. Instead, I stayed focused and swiftly made my way to the acoustic room. I was determined to get to the bottom of the Guitar Shop mystery once and for all. Fortunately, when I arrived at the acoustic room no other patrons were present. I had it all to myself just like old times.

I entered the room and was once more greeted by the refreshing sent of various woods, strings, and polishes. Talk about soothing for sore souls. It brought me instant peace and gratification. Then to my surprise directly across the room from me hanging on the wall as if it had been there all along there it was, Apollo's guitar.

At first, I thought my eyes were playing tricks on me. Could it really be? I sure hoped it was. Eager to verify the validity of my assumption I made way for the instrument. The closer I grew to it the realer it became. Then once it was in my hands there was no denying it. I had finally found what I had sought.

Overwhelmed with joy I decided to play the beautiful instrument. I must have played six songs or so before I was interrupted. I had begun to play "A hard rain is going to fall" by Bob Dylan. It was then when coincidentally an older man that resembled Bob Dylan overheard my playing and made his way into the acoustic room to observe.

At the end of the song the older gentleman complimented my performance.

"Well you sure do make that song sound pleasant if I do say so myself," he suggested wearing an inviting grin.

"Oh, I did not see you there... but thanks old timer," I said being modest.

It was then while really taking a good look at the feller I acknowledged his resemblance to Bob

Dylan. At first, I was not going to say anything. However, considering I was under the impression that Bob Dylan had died as a young man I decided to complement the man's resemblance.

"You know... the funny thing is here I am playing one of Dylan's classics and then you show up," I said nodding waiting on the man's approval as if he had comprehended my implication.

"Yeah, well what's funny about that," The man asked?

"Well you know... you look like Dylan," I suggested. "Well an older version of him anyway," I went on.

"An older version you say," the man asked? "I guess that makes sense considering I am the old version of Dylan," the man went on. "Bob Dylan's the name and you are," He continued as he extended out his hand to officially greet me.

"Ha ha... real funny I guess I deserve that," I replied. "Michael Kingston is the name kind sir," I continued as my hand met his in reciprocation.

"Well Michael just call me Bob," the man suggested.

As bizarre as it sounds by this point, I was starting to get the impression that the man really thought he was Bob Dylan. Rather than entertain the notion I decided to confront him.

"Um... okay so your name is Bob, but you are not Bob Dylan correct," I asked in a skeptical tone?

"No, my name is Bob, and I am Bob Dylan," the man quick wittedly refuted.

"Well unfortunately sir if you are Bob Dylan, I hate to be the barrier of bad news but you died years ago in a motorcycle accident which means I am talking to a ghost," I suggested sarcastically. "However, I don't believe ghosts are supposed to age... which by the way if you are Bob you have done significantly," I continued.

"Boy you sure are a funny fellow," the man suggested. "Fact of the matter is I am in fact Bob Dylan and as far as the motorcycle accident well... I didn't die just took it as a sign to take a break that is all," He continued. "So, again... just call me Bob," The man went on as he reached up and grabbed a guitar from the wall.

I figured I would honor the man wishes as far as his name goes but I would be lying if I said I did not still have doubts that he was pulling my leg. Then that all changed when he began to play. As the chords to Mr. Tambourine Man serenaded my ears against my better judgment the man had begun to sound convincing.

Then when he began to sing there was no doubt left in my mind. Another miracle was taking place before my eyes. As he played, I happen to look over at the glass door to the acoustic room and noticed two big bodyguard looking men were guarding the door. It all made sense.

In that thought I let go and ceased the moment. I allowed myself to enjoy Bob sing his song. It was a magical experience. By the end of that song in my mind Bob Dylan had been resurrected from the grave.

I could not believe that for so many years I had thought he was dead. Now, here he was. Who would have thought it? Then of all places at that Guitar Shop. It must have had some sort of significant meaning behind it on the grand scheme of things and I anticipated knowing.

"Well are you convinced yet," Bob asked ending the momentary silence that filled the room at the end of his song.

The truth was I was more than convinced. I was blown away by the idea of it all. Then the actualization of it was unbelievable.

"I have to say I am convinced Bob," I assured. "I am also relieved to know you are still alive," I continued. "I can't wait to hear your new music," I went on.

"Well let's not jump the gun young one," Bob interjected in a modest tone. "However, I do have a show coming up this weekend and would love for you to come," He continued. "In fact, how would you feel about opening up for me," Bob suggested.

"Opening up for you," I asked?

"Yes... you know like sing a song or two before I come on stage," Bob explained.

"Well... to be honest I have never played in front of a crowd," I explained. "I... am not sure I would be able to," I continued before Bob chimed in.

"Michael I am going to be honest with you... I think you have what it takes" Bob insisted. "In fact, I know you have what it takes," He went on. "That guitar in your hands says so," Bob continued.

His words sort of caught me by surprise. Then I remembered where I was and the long journey I had went down to get there. It was then I realized it all led up to that moment. I had my guitar back and I had a stage now waiting for my arrival. With that in mind I accept the gesture.

"You know what Bob... I think you are right," I professed. "I do have what it takes," I went on. "I would be honored to open up for you man," I continued as I extended my hand to seal the offer with a gentleman's shake.

"Great, glad you have decided to follow your fate," Bob said as he handed me a card with the details. "Be here and don't be late," Bob went on as he stood to his feet to leave.

As he neared the door to exit the acoustic room, he turned back to me and made a final statement.

"By the way... Do not think you are the only one who knows about the magic of this here room."

Then he gave a wink, a hysterical chuckle and proceeded to leave.

I knew my life had changed. I had finally realized who I was and what I was to do. I anxiously took the guitar I had searched high and low for to the counter to check out. When I arrived, Max was waiting grinning ear to ear.

"Well Michael I am glad you finally came back in and I see you found your guitar," Max said.

"Yeah I believe I have," I replied. "How much do I owe you," I asked?

"Actually... nothing," Max said in a compassionate tone. "Bob took care of it for you, so you are all set," Max went on. "I guess you made some impression on him, He continued.

"Well then now that's something... I guess I did," I said. "Well I guess I will be on my way then," I continued.

"Okay Michael enjoy the guitar, Max said as I departed.

On the ride home I contemplated calling Jill. I wanted to share my experience with her but was not sure she would be accepting. I also wanted her and the girls to come to the concert to see me perform. Despite my insecurities I decided to call.

Unfortunately, as I suspected she did not pick up. Instead, she allowed the voice mail to pick up. I knew she was home because it was her day off, so I took the gesture as if she did not want to be bothered. I respected that. So rather than call back I left a voice message on the machine.

"Hey Jill, it is me... Michael, I know you probably don't want to be hearing from me, but I wanted to invite you and the girls to a concert I am performing at. I really would like you guys to be there it is kind of a big deal for me," I was able to make out before the phone was deliberately forced to hang up.

I took that as a sign she did not want to be bothered and not to expect her to show up to the concert. I guess that was expected given the circumstance. Despite that I decided to write out the location and instructions and left it in her mailbox. I figured it was a long shot but just maybe a chance.

The days leading up to the concert I got better acquainted with my guitar. I must have played my set over a thousand times. I wanted to make sure I was going to be a success. Boy did my persistence pay off.

I arrived at the venue early the night of for set checks. Everything was on track for a big night. I tried to get in to see Bob, but he had his own ritual before shows. I guess I was not invited to that.

Instead, I started my own ritual. I prayed. Then I prayed again. Momentarily my nerves were getting the best of me. However, by the time they called five minutes to live my adrenaline kicked in and I was filled with confidence.

I grabbed my guitar said one last prayer and headed to the stage. I could hear the crowd going wild. I know they were cheering for Bob, but I pretended like it was for me. As I stood side stage waiting to go on being introduced by the host Bob came up behind me.

"Well hey Michael how does it feel," he asked as he threw his arm around my shoulder?

"Honestly, Bob this is something," I replied. I can see how this lifestyle can be very addictive," I went on.

"Yeah well try not to get addicted," Bob said as the host called me out to the stage. "Now go get them already," He went on as he gave my back a couple of pats.

As I walked out on to the stage the crowd roar sounded like thunder. It truly was an experience like no other. When I stepped to the microphone the roar subsided.

"Thank you so much.... I am going to sing Redemption Song by Bob Marley... I hope you all enjoy it," I announced as I began to play.

By the end of the song the crowd had determined I was a sensation. So, I went right into my next song.

"This next song is by Neil Young and it is called "Old Man", I announced, and the crowd roared as I began to play.

By the end of that song the crowd was chanting my name. I could not believe how loved I was. It gave me more confidence than I could have ever imagined having. I knew I was where I was supposed to be.

Then as I announced my final song, I noticed over standing by Bob was Jill and the girls. The sight of them filled me with joy. I could not take my eyes off them.

"This final song I am going to sing is called Fast Car by Tracy Chatman," I made out before the arena filled with a rumbling cheer. As I began to play my song Jill yelled out.

"We love you sweetheart... I love you," Jill professed.

I played that song as if my life depended on it. In a way in my mind it did because I was trying to win the confidence of my family back. By the end of that song I believe I did just that. Jill and the girls ran out on stage as I strummed the final chords.

When they made it to me at center stage, I swung my guitar behind me and took them all into my arms. As I embraced them, I yelled out to the crowd who were now going ecstatic at the site of our reunion.

"Everyone this is my family!" "I love them with all of my heart," I continued. "Thank you all so much for being a wonderful audience and have a great night," I went on.

As Jill the girls and I exited the stage I heard the crowd yelling out for an encore. I could not believe my ears. Nor could Bob.

"My god Michael you are a natural my boy," He said as we approached him. "Do you hear that... they cannot get enough of you," He went on.

"Yeah... I see," I said excited by all the commotion.

"Well you cannot just leave them hanging give them one more," Bob suggested.

"One more," I asked?

"Yes... get out there and give them what they want," Bob suggested encouragingly.

"Yes babe... go give them one more," Jill Concurred.

"Okay... I got one more... This one is for you," I said as I kissed Jill then headed back out to center stage.

The crowd went wild to see me back on stage. I could feel the rumble of their cheers throughout my entire body.

"Well I guess you all want one more," I asked the crowd?

They went wild to show their desire.

"Well... this song is dedicated to the love of my life. Baby this one is for you," I said as I began to play "All you need is love".

The crowd was so moved by my performance that halfway through the song we all began to sing it together.

Open

My Mind

My Heart

My Body

My Soul

I open their doors for you to explore:

I encourage you to do so with the intent that they

will be yours:

Marvel at their splendor and embrace their lore:

Intertwine in their genius:

Trust and believe their score:

Take refuge upon their shores:

For it is there homage is bestowed upon you where they besiege you to stay...

There, in their presence and in their comfort:

Where their compassion and understanding illume:

Your Mind

Your Heart

Your Body

Your Soul

So that they too shall be for me...

Open

LaVeL Regine

lavel.uk